MW01347066

Game for ADVENTURE

Andrew the Seeker

A GRAPHIC NOVEL

Lee Nordling & Scott Roberts

Graphic Universe™ · Minneapolis

For Cheri,
the love of all of my lives.
- Lee Nordling

To Copper,
the corgi who sat at my feet all the time I was working on this book.
- Scott Roberts

Lee Nordling is a two-time Eisner Award nominee and award-winning writer, editor, creative director, and book packager. He worked on staff at Disney Publishing, DC Comics, and *Nickelodeon Magazine*.

Scott Roberts is a two-time Eisner and Ignatz Award nominee, graphic novel artist and writer, illustrator, character designer, script doctor, and colorist. He's the creator of the comic book *Patty Cake*, a writer/artist for *Spongebob Comics*, draws the syndicated comics *Working Daze and Maria's Day*, and colors the classic Sunday comic *Prince Valiant*. Scott worked on the *Rugrats* comic strip with Lee Nordling.

Story and script by Lee Nordling
Art by Scott Roberts

Andrew the Seeker and the *Game for Adventure* series were placed, designed, and produced by The Pack.

Graphic Universe™ is a trademark of Lerner Publishing Group, Inc.

Graphic Universe™
A division of Lerner Publishing Group, Inc.
241 First Avenue North
Minneapolis, MN 55401 USA

For reading levels and more information, look up this title at www.lernerbooks.com.

Library of Congress Cataloging-in-Publication Data

Names: Nordling, Lee, author. | Roberts, Scott, illustrator.
Title: Andrew the seeker / Lee Nordling ; illustrated by Scott Roberts.
Description: Minneapolis : Graphic Universe, [2017] | Series: Game for adventure | Summary: "In this wordless graphic novel, Andrew sets out on a game of hide-and-seek with a friendly forest monster. Andrew is so focused—and the monster is so tricky—that Andrew cannot find it even when it is hiding in plain sight" – Provided by publisher.
Identifiers: LCCN 2016009479 (print) | LCCN 2016032634 (ebook) | ISBN 9781512413304 (lb : alk. paper) | ISBN 9781512430677 (pbk.) | ISBN 9781512427035 (eb pdf)
Subjects: LCSH: Graphic novels. | CYAC: Graphic novels. | Games—Fiction. | Hide-and-seek—Fiction. | Monsters—Fiction. | Stories without words.
Classification: LCC PZ7.7.N67 An 2017 (print) | LCC PZ7.7.N67 (ebook) | DDC 741.5/973—dc23

LC record available at https://lccn.loc.gov/2016009479

Manufactured in the United States of America
1-39788-21325-7/11/2016

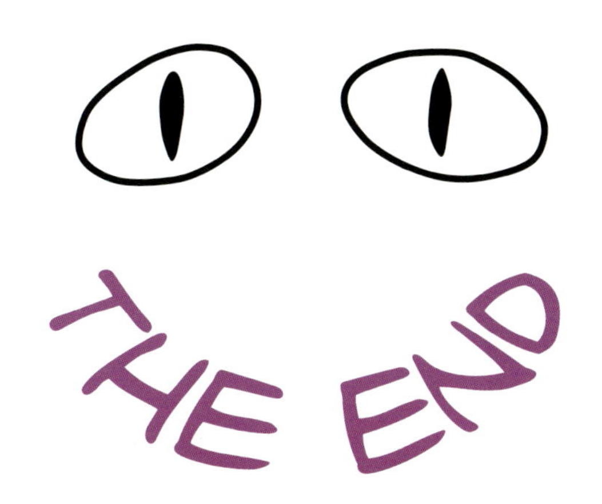
THE END

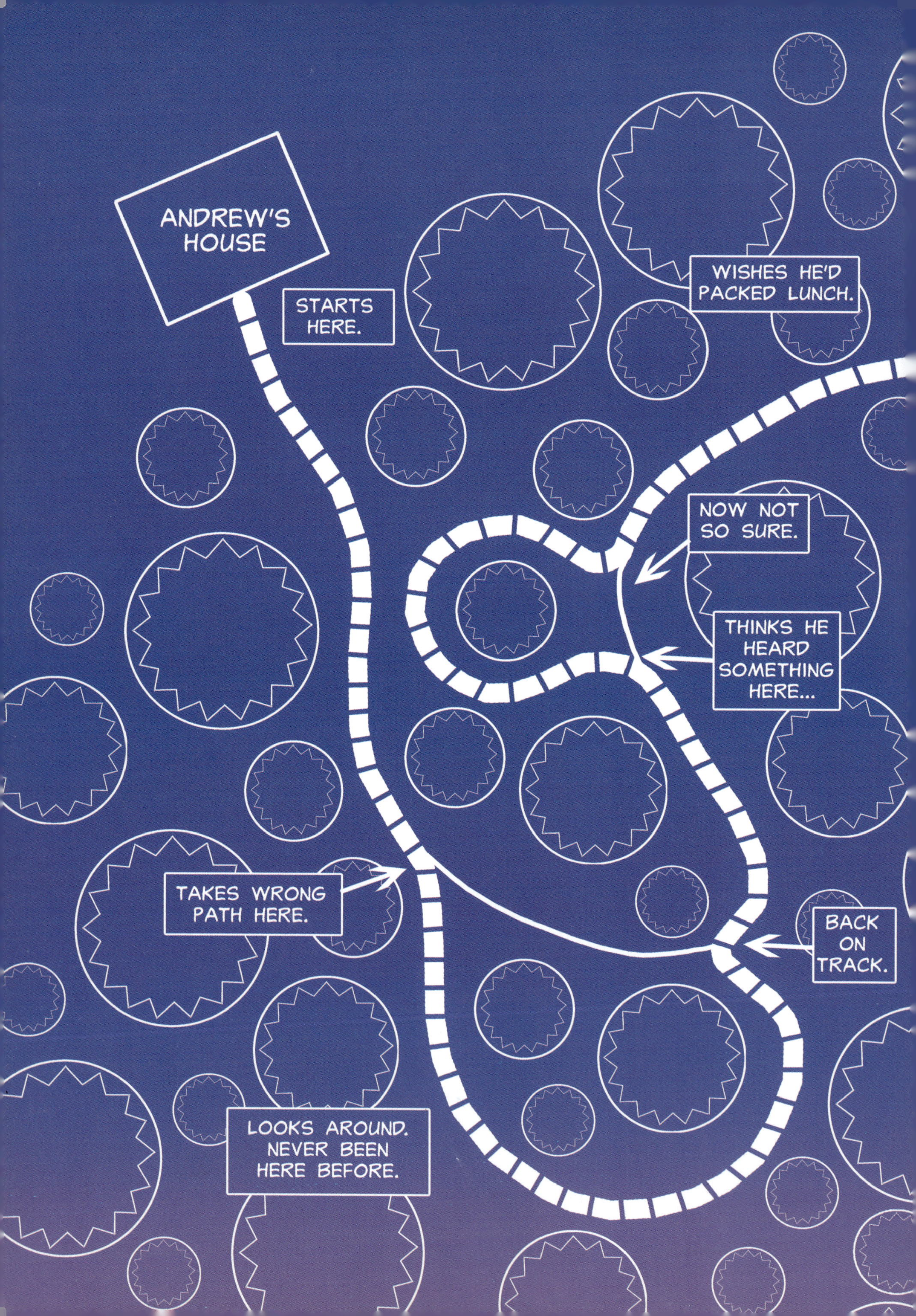
ANDREW'S HOUSE
STARTS HERE.
WISHES HE'D PACKED LUNCH.
NOW NOT SO SURE.
THINKS HE HEARD SOMETHING HERE...
TAKES WRONG PATH HERE.
BACK ON TRACK.
LOOKS AROUND. NEVER BEEN HERE BEFORE.

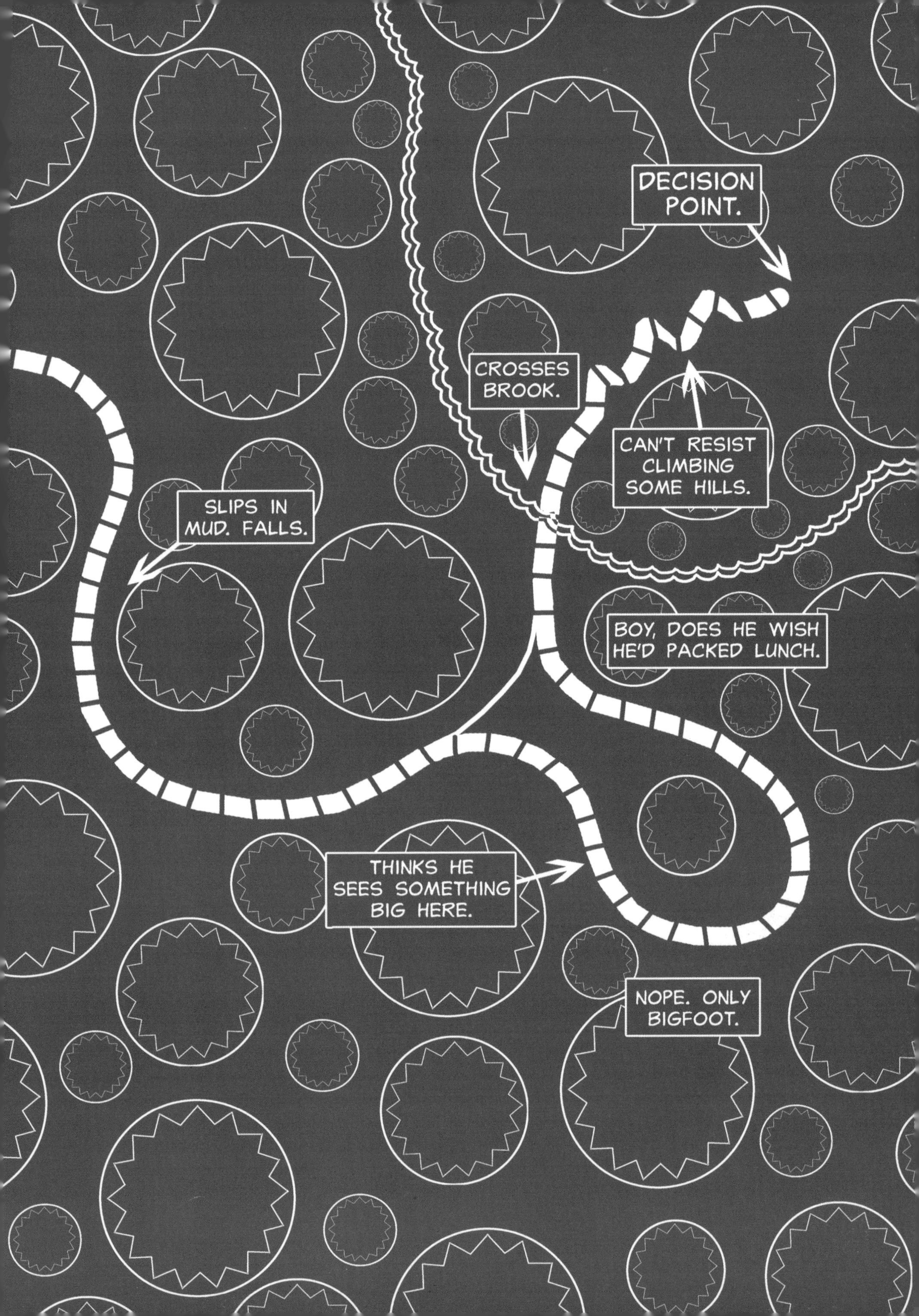
SLIPS IN MUD. FALLS.
CROSSES BROOK.
CAN'T RESIST CLIMBING SOME HILLS.
DECISION POINT.
BOY, DOES HE WISH HE'D PACKED LUNCH.
THINKS HE SEES SOMETHING BIG HERE.
NOPE. ONLY BIGFOOT.